This Walker book belongs to:

_____

_____

_____

This is the Kiss

Claire Harcup

Illustrated by Gabriel Alborozo

WALKER BOOKS
AND SUBSIDIARIES
LONDON · BOSTON · SYDNEY · AUCKLAND

When you've had a fun day
and you're ready for bed,

this is the wave ...

and the squeeze of the hand ...

that led to the touch ...

that led to the smile ...

that led to the hands going
round and round and round until ...

they started the tickle ...

that led to the wriggle ...

that led to the giggle ...

that led to the hug ...

that led to
the kiss
goodnight.

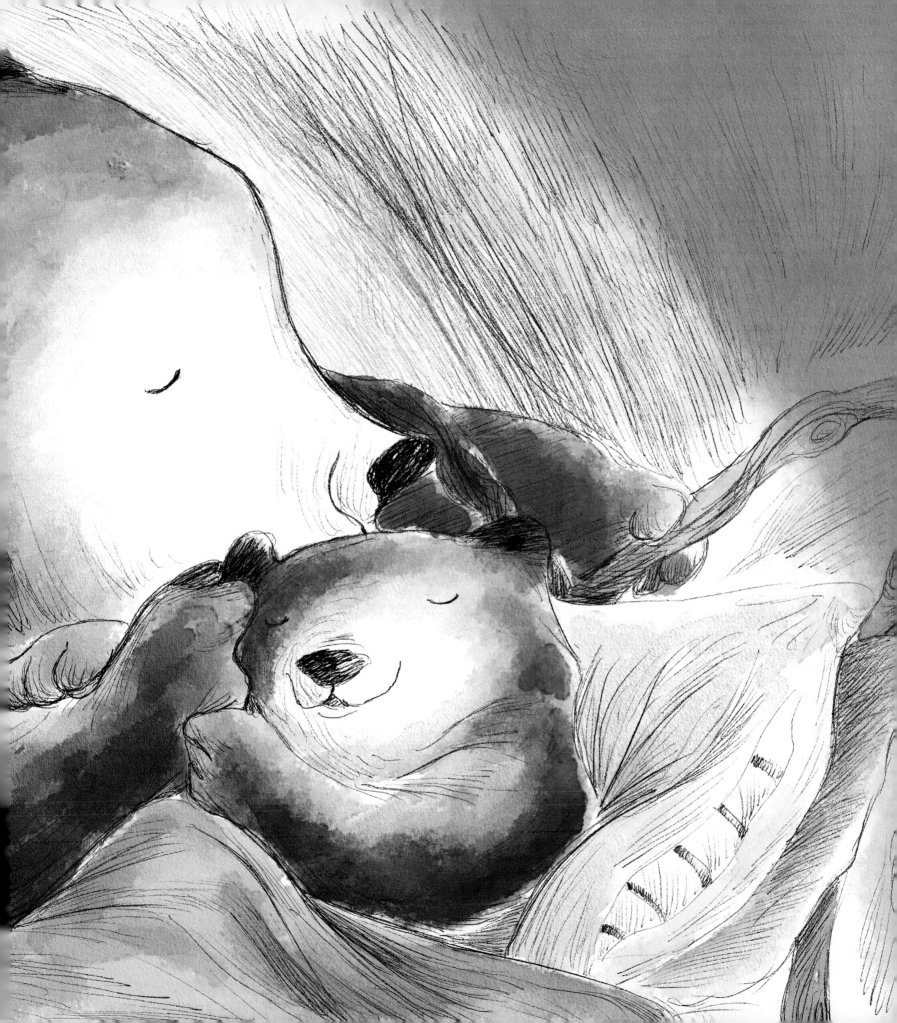

Sweet dreams